봄날 오후, 과부 셋

아시아에서는 《바이링궐 에디션 한국 대표 소설》을 기획하여 한국의 우수한 문학을 주제별로 엄선해 국내외 독자들에게 소개합니다. 이 기획은 국내외 우수한 번역가들이 참여하여 원작의 품격을 최대한 살렸습니다. 문학을 통해 아시아의 정체성과 가치를 살피는 데 주력해 온 아시아는 한국인의 삶을 넓고 깊게 이해하는 데 이 기획이 기여하기를 기대합니다..

Asia Publishers presents some of the very best modern Korean literature to readers worldwide through its new Korean literature series ⟨Bilingual Edition Modern Korean Literature⟩. We are proud and happy to offer it in the most authoritative translation by renowned translators of Korean literature. We hope that this series helps to build solid bridges between citizens of the world and Koreans through a rich in-depth understanding of Korea.

바이링궐 에디션 한국 대표 소설 063

Bi-lingual Edition Modern Korean Literature 063

Spring Afternoon, Three Widows

정지아
봄날 오후, 과부 셋

Jeong Ji-a

ASIA
PUBLISHERS

Contents

봄날 오후, 과부 셋

Spring Afternoon, Three Widows

봄바람이 앙탈하는 아이처럼 마당을 휩쓴다. 어지간한 바람에는 끄덕도 않던 남보라 빛 수국마저 미친년 널뛰듯 몸을 뒤챈다. 간신히 매달려 있던 무거운 꽃송이가 뚝 부러질 것만 같다. 가만 보니 그것은 수국이 아니라 빨랫줄에서 펄럭거리는 남보라 빛 치마다. 요즘은 자꾸 헛것이 보인다. 헛것이 보인다고 한숨결에 한마디 했더니만 서울 사는 딸년은 짜증스럽게 헛것은 무슨, 백내장이 심해 그렇지, 무안하게 쏘아붙였다. 썩을 년. 딸 말이 맞을 것이다. 그러나 백태 낀 눈이 빚어내는 착각이 그녀에게는 잠시의 현실이다. 그녀는 보송보송 마른 빨래를 걷는다. 반나절 만에 빨래를 말린 성급한 바

A spring gust swept through the courtyard like a bad-tempered child. The hydrangea, steady in a normal wind, shook violently like a deranged woman on a seesaw. The heavy hydrangea flowers hung on for dear life; it seemed as if they would break off at any moment. After a second look, the woman realized that it wasn't the hydrangea shaking; it was the blue-violet skirt flapping on her clothesline. These days she was troubled by phantoms. But when she mentioned phantoms to her daughter in Seoul, she was met with nothing but the inconsiderate retort: "Phantoms! Nonsense, it's probably just your worsening cataracts."

람처럼 그녀의 80년도 순식간에 지나가버렸다. 누군가 그녀의 세월 밖에서 그녀의 한 삶을 지켜보고 있다가 빨래를 걷듯 목숨줄을 획 걷어버리는 것인지도 모른다, 삶이란 것은.

"잘도 말랐네."

혼잣말을 중얼거리며 그녀는 마루에 앉아 옷을 개킨다. 옷이라고 해봐야 월남치마와 양말 몇 짝, 아직도 벗지 못한 겨울내의뿐이다. 젊은 날 그녀는 어떤 옷이든 하루 이상 입지 않았다. 늙으니 만사가 귀찮다. 겨울에는 같은 옷을 일주일씩도 입는다. 기름기가 없어 그런지 일주일씩 입어도 더러움을 타지 않는다. 젊은 날, 그녀의 피부는 건조한 한겨울에도 자르르 기름기가 돌았다. 그 기름진 살결은 세월 속에서 차츰 기름기를 잃어 언젠가부터 푸석푸석 살비듬이 일었다. 매일 아침 방바닥에 떨어진 살비듬을 손으로 쓸면 손바닥이 온통 허옜다. 살비듬이 빠져나간 생명이나 되는 양 그녀는 아침마다 심란하다.

"뭐하요?"

대서소 김 영감이 문밖에서 비죽 얼굴을 들이밀며 묻는다. 그녀보다 두 살 아래인 김 영감은 아직도 대서소

The miserable girl was probably right. The illusions created by her cataracts were a momentary reality. Her eighty years flashed by like the gust of the wind that had dried her clothes in only half a day. She took the wash off the line. Maybe an observer from outside of time was hauling in her lifeline like she was taking in her wash. *That's life.*

"Nicely dry," she said. She sat up onto the porch and folded her clothes: A winter skirt, a few pairs of socks and the heavy winter underwear she still wore—nothing else. In her younger days, she'd changed her outfit every day. Now, everything was a headache. In the winter, she wore the same clothes for a week. Could be the lack of sap; even a week's wear didn't soil her clothes.

In her youth, her skin had glowed, even in the dry cold days of winter. Over time, her supple skin had gradually lost its sheen, a scaly flakiness taking its place. Every morning, she wiped the flakes of skin off the floor with her hand – her palm caked white. Those white flakes, as if a testament to her life on the slide, spoiled her mornings.

"What are you up to?" Kim the old notary officer asked, poking his head around the yard door. He was two years her junior and still working. Running

를 한다. 돈이야 몇 푼 벌릴까만 그냥 심심풀이로 하는 눈치다. 요 몇 년 전부터 김 영감은 아침저녁으로 오며 가며 문안인사를 한다.

"남이사 뭘 하든!"

김 영감을 그녀는 한 번도 문 안에 들이지 않았다. 남자가 그리울 나이도 아니고, 이 나이에 괜스레 정이라도 주었다가는 젊어서의 영욕이 눈덩이처럼 불어 되돌아올 것이다.

"수국이 참 예뻐요."

싱거운 말을 던져놓고 김 영감은 사라진다. 마당 한구석에 수국이 소담스레 피어 있다. 30여 년 전 하루꼬네집에서 한 뿌리 얻어다 심어놓은 것이 어느새 마당 한켠을 점령했다. 그러고 보니 하루꼬가 오지 않았다. 지난 두 해 동안 아침참이 지나면 어김없이 대문간을 들어서던 하루꼬다. 비가 오거나 눈이 오거나 거르는 법이 없어 적잖이 귀찮아하던 그녀는 허둥지둥 문을 나선다. 옆집 조 여사는 지난겨울 웃으며 인사하고 헤어진지 한 시간 만에 뇌출혈로 목숨줄을 놓았다. 여든쯤 되면 언제 불려갈지 10분을 기약할 수 없는 법이다. 급한 걸음으로 성당 앞을 지나는데 저만치 하루꼬가 목을 축

a notary office kept him occupied though there was very little money in it. In recent years, he'd taken to looking in on her on his way to and from work.

"None of your business," she said.

She never allowed Kim inside the door. Too old now to be interested in men, thoughts of love at her age would just inflame past passions.

"The hydrangeas are pretty," Kim said flatly and disappeared.

The hydrangeas were blooming perfectly in a corner of the yard. Thirty years ago she'd planted a slip from Haruko's garden, and before long it took over part of the yard. Haruko hadn't come yet. For the past two years, after the breakfast lull, Haruko had appeared at the door every day. Rain or snow made no difference; it was annoying. But she was worried now that Haruko hadn't shown up and so she hustled out of the yard. Last winter, an hour after a final smiling visit, Granny Cho next door had been stricken by a brain hemorrhage. In your eighties, you couldn't predict the timing of your final call.

As she rushed past the front of the church, Haruko appeared, neck outstretched goose-like and

늘어뜨린 채 흐느적흐느적 걸어오고 있다. 하루꼬의 무심한 시선은 그녀를 사물인 양 스쳐 지난다.

"하루꼬!"

몇 걸음이나 지나쳐 가버린 하루꼬가 제 이름 부르는 소리에 걸음을 멈춘다. 다행히 아직은 온정신인 모양이다. 하루꼬는 돌봐줄 자식 하나 없다.

"왜 이렇게 늦었어?"

"응, 영감 아침상이 늦어서. 배가 안 고프다고 거르겠다잖아. 그래 기어이 한숟갈 먹이느라 늦었지."

하루꼬의 영감은 2년 전 이맘때 세상을 떴다. 남편이 죽은 뒤에도 하루꼬는 하루도 거르지 않고 남편 상을 봤다. 어제는 저는 먹지도 않는 육회를 차려놓고, 영감 죽기 몇 년 전부터 고기 썰기 귀찮아 그 좋아하는 육회 한 번 해주지 않았다고 종일 눈물바람이었다. 그랬어도 살아 있는 남편 밥상을 챙겼노라고 한 적은 한 번도 없었다. 아무래도 하루꼬가 이상하다. 언젠가 이런 날이 올 줄 알았다.

마루에 엉덩이를 걸치기 무섭게 눈물을 짜던 하루꼬가 오늘은 웬일로 무심히 수국을 바라본다. 하루꼬는 어려서부터 수국을 좋아했다. 그녀는 수국이 싫었다.

staggering along. Haruko's indifferent glance at her was one of total non-recognition.

"Haruko!"

At the sound of her name, Haruko stopped a few paces ahead of her. Fortunately, she appeared okay. She had no children to look after.

"What's kept you?"

"Ah, the old man wouldn't have breakfast, said he wasn't hungry. I had to spoon-feed him, that held me up."

Haruko's husband had died two years ago. Thereafter, she never failed to prepare his breakfast table. Yesterday, she'd served raw beef, a dish she didn't like herself. Today, she'd been in tears of self-recrimination: she was fed up cutting meat. She hadn't prepared his favorite dish for years before his death, although she'd never confused the table setting when he was alive, either. Haruko was strange. The other woman knew this day was inevitable.

Haruko, who'd lain spread-eagle on the porch in a flood of tears, today just stared vacantly at the hydrangeas. Haruko had liked hydrangeas when she was young. The woman could not abide them. Lopsided, large purplish flowers, drooping lan-

멋대가리 없이 꽃송이만 커다래서 힘없이 축 늘어진 게 음습한 남보라 빛하며 도무지 정이 가질 않았다. 그래도 수국이 흐드러지는 오뉴월이면 하루꼬네 집에 갈 때마다 몇 송이 꺾어가곤 했다. 열네 살 하루꼬는 그 꽃을 유리병에 꽂아놓고는 앉은뱅이책상에 턱을 괸 채 그녀의 존재조차 까맣게 잊고 무심히 꽃만 바라보았다.

"나는 수국이 싫어! 꼭 눈물 같잖아."

그녀는 수국으로만 향한 하루꼬의 오롯한 시선이 샘이 나서 괜스레 트집을 잡았다. 그때처럼 하루꼬는 수국만 바라본다. 그녀는 하루꼬의 팔을 잡아 일으켰다. 오늘은 같이 갈 데가 있다.

"하루꼬, 사다꼬네 가자."

"사다꼬?"

"그래, 사다꼬. 우리 동창 사다꼬."

그녀들은 읍내에 하나밖에 없던 보통학교 동창이다. 어려서 만나 일본 이름으로 부르기 시작한 탓에 아직도 일본 이름이 더 친숙하다. 그녀의 이름은 영자지만 친구들에게 그녀는 되바라진 에이꼬다.

"나 그런 사람 몰라."

여전히 수국을 응시한 채로 하루꼬는 고개를 젓는다.

guidly and shapelessly—hydrangeas failed utterly to stir any feeling in her. In the old days, when the hydrangeas were in full bloom during the sunny months of May and June, she would cut a few blossoms and take them along on every visit to Haruko's house. Haruko, only fourteen at the time, would put the flowers in a bottle on a low table, cupping her hands to her chin and staring vacantly at the flowers. She would forget her friend's existence completely.

"I hate hydrangeas. The petals are like tears."

She was nitpicking needlessly, jealous of the way Haruko looked at the flowers. In her younger days, Haruko had eyes only for hydrangeas. The other woman took her arm and raised her to her feet. They had a common goal today.

"Haruko, let's go to Sadako's."

"Sadako?"

"Yes, Sadako, our classmate."

They had been in the same class in the town's only elementary school. They used Japanese names then, and those names were still more familiar to them. She was Youngja, but to her two friends she was prissy Aiko.

"I don't know her," Haruko said, shaking her

사다꼬를 모르다니. 그럴 리가 없다. 하루꼬는 사다꼬
와 단짝이었다. 그녀만 쏙 빼고 자기들끼리 몰래 어울
려 다닌 것도 그녀는 알고 있었다. 샘 많은 그녀가 샘이
나 토라진 적도 골백번이었다.

"꿀 먹은 벙어리 사다꼬 말이야."

언젠가부터 죽으면 죽었지 어떻게 잊을까 싶었던 일
을 까맣게 잊기도 하고, 까맣게 잊었던 일을 느닷없이
기억하기도 했다. 기껏 잘 숨겨놓은 통장을 도무지 찾
지 못한 적도 있다. 잘 숨겨진 통장처럼 사다꼬의 기억
도 하루꼬의 머릿속 어딘가 곱게 숨어 있을 것이다. 무
언가 실마리를 찾기만 하면 쉰내 나도록 묵은 기억이
실타래처럼 풀려나올지도 모른다.

"기억나? 결혼하기 며칠 전날 사다꼬가 너희 집에 와
서 눈이 퉁퉁 붓도록 울었잖아."

하루꼬도 말수가 적었지만 사다꼬에게는 멜 게 아니
었다. 남자들을 젖히고 늘 1등이던 사다꼬는 먼저는 입
을 떼는 법이 없었고, 누가 뭘 물어도 응, 아니, 단답형
의 대답밖에 하지 않았다. 아이들은 사다꼬로부터 가장
긴 대답을 얻어내는 사람에게 모찌 사주기 따위의 내기
로 어린 날의 지루한 시간을 흘려보냈다. 사다꼬는 공

head, her eyes transfixed by the hydrangeas. She doesn't know Sadako, Aiko thought. Impossible. Sadako and Haruko were bosom pals. Aiko knew how they liked to steal off to be by themselves. She was a very jealous woman, and the conduct of her friends often led her to sulk.

"Sadako the dummy. Of course you know her."

Recently, Aiko had begun to forget things she thought she'd never forget, not even in death, and out of the blue she'd begun to remember things she thought she'd completely forgotten. Once she couldn't find a bank deposit book that she'd carefully put away. Like that hidden bank book Haruko's memory of Sadako was tucked away safely in her head. And in the same way a thread unravels when you find where it starts, Haruko's hidden memory looked like it might also unravel in time.

"Sadako came to your house a few days before her wedding and cried her heart out. You remember, surely?"

Haruko was a girl of few words but she was no match for Sadako in reticence. Sadako beat all the smartest boys in contest, but she never opened her mouth first. Her only responses to any questions asked of her: yes and no. The students spent their

부 잘하고 얌전한 데다 인물까지 반반해서 선생님과 남자 동창들의 사랑을 한 몸에 받았다. 누가 무슨 말을 해도 꿀 먹은 벙어리로 삼키기만 하고 여간해서는 내뱉는 법이 없어 여자애들에게도 인기가 좋았다. 사다꼬에게 말한 비밀은 절대 새는 법이 없었으니까. 단짝으로 붙어 다녔지만 그녀는 누구에게나 인기 좋은 사다꼬가 꼭 좋지만은 않았다. 사다꼬가 동경제대 나온 남자와 혼인하게 되었을 때도 그녀는 혼자서 몇 날 며칠 속을 끓였다. 그때 그녀는 김약방 박 조수와 막 혼인을 한 참이었다. 동경제대라는 말을 듣는 순간 몇 년이나 죽고 못 살았던 박 조수에 대한 마음이 깨끗이 가셨다. 그런 저에게 더 화가 나서 그녀는 눈이 퉁퉁 붓도록 울먹이는 사다꼬에게 동경제대가 싫어? 호강에 초쳤다, 기어이 비아냥거리고 말았다. 그날 새벽 사다꼬는 동경에 가서 고학을 하겠다며 부산행 열차에 올랐다. 다시 잡혀와 머리 박박 밀린 채 결국 시집을 가기는 했지만.

"사다꼬…… 사다꼬……."

하루꼬가 사다꼬의 이름을 몇 번이나 입 안에서 궁굴렸다. 그래도 기억은 돌아오지 않는 모양이었다.

"나 그런 사람 몰라."

dull school days betting sticky rice cakes on who could get the longest response from Sadako. Along with being gentle and having brains to spare, Sadako was attractive and loved by all the teachers and boys in her class. She swallowed everything she heard—like a dummy who'd gotten the best honey, and, she was so excellent at not divulging what she heard that she was popular with the girls too. With Sadako, a secret was leak-proof.

Although a close friend of hers, Aiko sometimes felt envious of Sadako's popularity. When word got out that Sadako was to be married to a graduate of the prestigious Tokyo Imperial University, Aiko spent days in inner turmoil. She had just married Park, an assistant in Kim's Pharmacy, but years of love for Park vanished when she heard about Sadako's TIU graduate.

It was probably anger that prompted Aiko's sarcasm towards Sadako. Sadako's eyes were swollen from tears. She asked her if it was TIU she disliked or if she had something against luxury.

Early the next morning Sadako took the Busan train to get to Tokyo, insisting she was going to become a working student. She was arrested and ended up with a close-cropped head on the day of

"모르긴 왜 몰라! 사다꼬를."

울컥 속이 상해서 그녀는 버럭 소리를 질렀다.

"일어서!"

그녀는 하루꼬의 팔을 부여잡고 성큼성큼 걸음을 옮겼다. 도살장에 끌려가는 소처럼 하루꼬는 미적미적 그녀의 뒤를 따랐다. 어려서부터 하루꼬는 늘 그랬다. 그녀가 김약방을 기웃거리던 무렵 하루꼬는 급장이던 가네무라 에이이찌를 마음에 두었다. 물론 제 입으로 말한 적은 없었다. 그래도 하루꼬가 에이이찌를 좋아한다는 사실을 반 전체가 다 알았다. 에이이찌가 근처에 오기만 해도 하루꼬의 하얀 뺨이 발갛게 달아올랐던 것이다. 그녀는 교정에 등꽃이 만발한 어느 초여름 밤, 하루꼬를 부추겨 장문의 연애편지를 쓰게 했다. 쓰기는 하루꼬가 썼으나 저 혼자서는 한 문장도 만들지 못해 그녀가 옆에서 따박따박 읊어준 편지였다. 하루꼬가 새벽에 구겨버린 그 편지를 인두로 깨끗이 다려 에이이찌의 가방 속에 넣어둔 것은 그녀였다. 에이이찌는 방과 후 하루꼬를 등나무 아래로 불렀다. 얼굴이 홍옥처럼 붉어진 하루꼬는 가방도 놔둔 채 줄행랑을 놓았고, 그녀가 대신 등나무 밑 벤치로 나갔다. 누가 모범생 아니랄까봐,

her wedding.

"Sadako," Haruko mused, rolling the name around her mouth a few times but apparently without immediate recall.

"I don't know that name."

"How can you not know Sadako?" Aiko shouted, thoroughly agitated, "Get up!"

She grabbed hold of Haruko's arm and stalked away. Haruko staggered fitfully in her wake, as she always did in days past, like a haltered cow on the way to the slaughterhouse.

When Aiko had set her eye on Park from Kim's Pharmacy, Haruko set her mind on the class leader Kamaymura Aichi. Of course, Haruko had never said a word about her feelings, but the whole class knew she liked him. Her white cheeks flushed if Aichi appeared anywhere nearby.

Early one summer's night, when the schoolyard was awash with wisteria, Aiko made Haruko write a long love letter for her. Yes, Haruko wrote it, but not one sentence was crafted without Aiko's attentive ministrations. And it was Aiko who rolled Haruko's letter out with the iron—Haruko had crumpled it up into a ball at dawn—and then slipped it in Aichi's school bag. When Aichi found the letter,

"여자 행실이 이래서야 되겠어."

정색을 하고 훈계를 한 에이이찌는 하루꼬가 밤새워 쓴 편지를 돌려주었다.

"바보! 여자 마음도 모르는 게 공부는 잘해 무엇해."

그녀가 야무지게 쏘아붙이자 에이이찌는 어안이 벙벙하여 아무 말도 하지 못했다.

"너…… 혹시 다른 여자를 마음에 두고 있는 거야? 그래서 하루꼬가 싫은 거지? 맞지?"

이상한 예감에 그녀는 그렇게 몰아붙였고, 에이이찌는 황급히 그녀의 시선을 피했다. 친구들 중에 가장 빨라 열넷에 초경을 한 그녀는 그래서인지 동급생들보다 이성문제에 밝았다.

"혹시 사다꼬야?"

그녀는 내처 물었다. 등나무 터널을 통과한 초여름 오후의 햇살이 에이이찌의 얼굴 위에서 그물망처럼 어른거렸다. 에이이찌는 아무 말도 하지 않았다. 사다꼬가 분명했다.

"바보! 벙어리 사다꼬가 뭐가 좋다고!"

제 사랑이 끝난 것도 아닌데 그녀는 등나무 아래를 걸어 나오며 눈물을 질금거렸다. 아마 말 한 번 건네지

he summoned Haruko to the wisteria.

Haruko ran off, her face ruby red, leaving her bag behind her. Aiko took her place on the bench under the wisteria.

"How can a woman behave like this?" Aichi said pompously, his face reflecting his status as the class leader when he handed back the flattened, heavily lined letter.

"Fool! What's the point of all your studies when you don't even know the heart of a girl."

Aghast at Aiko's sharp rejoinder, Aichi was struck dumb.

"In love with someone else, is that it? That's why you dislike Haruko? Admit it!"

Thunderstruck by the strangely prescient attack, Aichi abruptly turned away from Aiko's unrelenting stare. She was quick at understanding boy-girl relations, probably because she was the first of the 14-year-olds to reach puberty.

"Sadako, huh?" Aiko persisted. A shaft of early summer afternoon sunlight—like a fishing net through the wisteria – illumined Aichi's face from above. He remained silent. Clearly, it was Sadako.

"Fool! What's so great about Sadako the dummy?"

It wasn't Aiko's love that had been blighted, but

못한 제 사랑이 감정 이입된 탓이었으리라. 달콤한 등나무꽃 향기가 그날은 달콤해서 더욱 서러웠다. 그 꽃향기며 햇살 어른거리던 에이이찌의 붉은 얼굴이 아직도 눈에 선하다.

"나는 싫어. 너 혼자 다녀와."

사다꼬의 집 앞에서 하루꼬는 또다시 멈칫거린다. 곡마단 구경을 갈 때도 밤벚꽃놀이를 갈 때도 어렵사리 꾀어놓으면 하루꼬는 곡마단 앞에서 혹은 꽃구경 가는 길에 미적미적 돌아서곤 했다. 팔십이 넘은 지금도 열네 살 시절과 똑같다. 전주사범 나온 선생과 혼인날을 받아놓고도 하루꼬는 볼살이 쏙 빠지도록 걱정이 태산이었다. 생판 모르는 사람과 어떻게 한 방에서 같이 사느냐고, 어떻게 어머니를 두고 가느냐고, 틈만 나면 질질 눈물을 짜던 하루꼬는 시집간 지 2년 만에 보얗게 살이 오른 채 친정에 다니러 왔고, 이번에는 혼자 두고 온 남편이 걱정이 되어 이틀 만에 부랴부랴 돌아갔다. 매번 새로운 것 앞에서 미적미적 망설이지만 함께한 시간만큼 깊이 마음을 주는 게 하루꼬다.

"얼굴 보면 기억이 날 거야. 들어가자."

곡마단 휘장 속으로 등을 떠밀듯 그녀는 늙은 하루꼬

when she came out from under the wisteria, her face was bathed in tears, probably due to her empathy for unrequited love the world over. The aroma of the sweet wisteria flowers, even more fragrant that afternoon, intensified her sorrow. The scent of the wisteria and Aichi's red, sunlight-illumined face were still fresh in her memory.

Haruko hesitated in front of Sadako's house.

"Go in on your own, I don't want to," she said.

When they went to the circus or to the cherry blossom festival at night, Haruko always baulked at the last minute. 80-year-olds were replicas of 14-year-olds. Even before Haruko wed the graduate from Jeonju Teachers' College—marrying into privilege—she was nothing but skin and bones, a ball of nerves. How could she live in such close quarters with a total stranger? How could she just leave her mother like this? Given the slightest opportunity, she burst into tears. Two years later and full of energy, she came back to her own house. But she was so concerned about her bereft husband that she bustled back to him two days later. For Haruko, everything new was a cause of fumbling hesitation that developed later into total devotion.

의 등을 떠민다. 문은 열려 있다. 오래된 쇠문이 요란한 소리를 내며 열리는데도 안에서는 인기척이 없다. 사다꼬는 낡아서 허물어질 듯한 연립에 산다. 이만한 집 한 채라도 건사하게 된 게 아마 환갑 지난 후였으리라. 들어오라는 허락도 없이 그녀는 마루에 올라선다. 아귀가 맞지 않은 안방 문을 힘껏 잡아당겼으나 안방에는 스산한 냉기뿐이다.

"사다꼬! 사다꼬!"

"으응, 누구야?"

거실의 눈부신 봄볕 속에서 희미한 목소리가 들린다. 아지랑이처럼 어룽거리는 빛 속에 사다꼬가 덩그마니 앉아 있다. 워낙 몸피가 적은 데다 빛이 어른거려 보이지 않았던 모양이다. 흐릿한 시선이 그녀를 향한다. 열넷의 사다꼬는 몸집이 작은 데다 유난히 눈빛이 반짝거려 생쥐 같았다. 세월이 눈빛의 총기를 야금야금 갉아먹고 총기 대신 흐릿한 백태를 끼워놓았으리라. 한참 후에야 그녀를 알아보고 몸을 일으키려던 사다꼬가 비그르르 바닥에 주저앉는다. 사다꼬를 부축하여 벽에 기대 앉힌 후 그녀는 여직 현관에서 머뭇거리는 하루꼬를 끌고 온다. 사다꼬의 눈에 반짝 생기가 돈다. 사다꼬가

"You'll remember when you see her face. Let's go inside."

Aiko pushed Haruko ahead as if goading her onto the circus stage from behind a tent flap. The house was unlocked. The old galvanized door squeaked open, but there was no movement inside. Sadako was living in an old, dilapidated flat. She'd probably bought the run-down place after her sixtieth birthday. Aiko stepped up onto the porch, though without any invitation from within. She gave a sharp tug on the bedroom door, which was hanging askew on its frame. The bedroom was ice cold.

"Sadako! Sadako!

"Yes, who's there?" A faint voice sounded from the living room, ablaze in spring sunlight.

Sadako sat in the shimmering light, small and alone. Tiny-framed and apparently blinded by the light, she stared dimly at Aiko. The 14-year-old Sadako had been like a mouse—tiny build, eyes that glimmered brightly. Life had gradually worn down those bright eyes and injected a cloudy film in their place.

After a moment, Sadako realized who was there. She attempted to get up but collapsed in a heap on the floor. Aiko propped her up against the wall,

덥석 하루꼬의 손을 잡는다. 난처한 기색으로 그녀를 바라보면서 하루꼬는 슬며시 손을 뺀다. 얼굴을 보고도 기억이 나지 않는 것이다. 영문을 알 리 없는 사다꼬가 어리둥절 그녀를 바라본다.

"얘가 지지난해 영감을 보낸 후로 왔다 갔다 한다. 오늘은 더 하네."

"그 양반이 갔어? 나는 그것도 몰랐네. 기별이라도 하지 왜."

영감을 보내놓고 하루꼬는 누구에게 기별할 정신조차 없었다. 하루꼬는 나 좀 데려가라고, 왜 영감 혼자 갔느냐고 악을 쓰며 울다 몇 번이나 정신을 잃었다. 자식도 없는 데다 하루꼬나 그 남편이나 서점에 틀어박혀 주위 사람들과 별로 어울리지 않은 탓에 장례식장은 쓸쓸하기 짝이 없었다. 유일한 상주인 하루꼬는 영안실에 오기만 하면 혼절을 하고, 염이며 입관이며 화장이며 모든 절차를 그녀가 도맡아 처리했다. 하루꼬의 뒤처리를 그녀가 하게 될 줄은 몰랐다. 하루꼬나 사다꼬는 저희들끼리는 곧잘 속을 털어놓는 눈치였지만 그녀에게는 한 번도 속엣말을 하지 않았다. 하루꼬 남편이 잘 다니던 학교를 때려치우고 낙향하게 된 이유도 하루꼬의

then drew Haruko inside; Haruko had been fumbling around outside. Sadako's eyes lit up momentarily. Abruptly, she grabbed Haruko's hand. Haruko looked at Aiko awkwardly and withdrew. Sadako's face did not prompt any recall. Sadako looked at Haruko in puzzlement.

"Haruko loses it sometimes, ever since she buried her husband two years ago. She's worse today. She says she doesn't know you."

"Her husband died? I had no idea. Why wasn't I notified?"

Haruko hadn't been able to alert anyone about her husband's passing. She had lost her wits completely. "Take me with you; why are you going on your own?" she cried, making a scene.

The funeral was unparalleled in loneliness, probably because they were childless and because they stuck to themselves in the bookstore, hardly ever engaging with their neighbors. Haruko was the chief mourner but she fainted every time she went to the mortuary. Everything fell to Aiko: the ritual preparation of the corpse, laying out the coffin, and seeing to the cremation. She was so busy looking after Haruko that she was unable to send notices of Haruko's husband's death.

입을 통해서는 들은 적이 없다. 샌님 같이 생긴 하루꼬의 남편이 전교조라나 뭐라나, 4·19 뒤에 세상 좋아진 줄 알고 괜히 설쳤다가 쫓겨났다는 사실을 무슨 말 끝에 사다꼬에게 들었다. 그때 사다꼬와 하루꼬는 서로 먹고살기 바빠 왕래도 뜸했다. 거의 매일 보는 그녀도 모르는 하루꼬의 비밀을 사다꼬는 알고 있었다. 그럴수록 그녀는 하루꼬를 챙겼다. 쉰쯤 되었을 때 하루꼬는 무슨 큰 비밀이라도 털어놓듯 첫아이 가졌을 때 잘못되어 자궁을 들어내는 바람에 다시는 아이를 가질 수 없게 되었노라고 울먹이며 털어놓았다. 40년 공을 들여 처음 얻은 수확이었다. 다음 장날 약방에 들른 사다꼬에게 자랑하듯 그 이야기를 속닥였더니 사다꼬는 저만치 나무의자에 앉아 기다리는 손님들을 긴장하여 휘 둘러보고는, 다시는 그 얘기 입에도 담지 말라고, 자칫 소문이라도 나면 하루꼬가 혀 깨물고 죽어버릴지도 모른다고, 그녀 가슴에 비수를 박았다. 사다꼬는 진작 알고 있었다. 저희들 둘이서는 안 하는 이야기 없이 종알거렸던 것이다. 그럴수록 그녀는 기를 쓰고 하루꼬에게 잘 했다. 그래 봤자 늘 무덤덤, 가면 반기고 돌아서면 잘 가라고 인사하던 하루꼬가 변하기 시작한 것은 제 남편

Aiko didn't know she'd have to mind Haruko afterwards. There was a ready willingness for Haruko and Sadako to talk things out together, but Haruko never once unburdened herself privately to Aiko.

Haruko hadn't told Aiko why her husband had quit teaching and returned home. Aiko heard about it later from Sadako. A meek man, someone who ardently believed that the world had changed for the better after the 1960 student uprising, he was fired for active involvement in an illegal radical teachers group. At that time, Sadako and Haruko were so busy with their own lives that they were rarely in touch with each other. Aiko was used to seeing Haruko almost daily, but she was ignorant of the inner secrets that were for Sadako's ears only. This actually spurred her on to take care of Haruko.

Once when Haruko was about fifty, she broke down in tears. With the air of someone about to disclose something deeply private, she told Aiko about her first pregnancy, how she had had a miscarriage, and how further pregnancies were out of the question. That was their first heart-to-heart in 40 years.

When Aiko proudly whispered the story to Sada-

이 죽은 뒤부터였다. 남편을 잃은 하루꼬는 온전히 그녀에게 기댔다. 사다꼬 같은 건 기억조차 하지 못한다.

"얘가 워낙 정신이 없어서…… 영감 보내놓고 저도 가게 생겼다. 오늘은 영감 아침밥 먹이느라 우리 집에 늦게 왔다고 하더라니까. 너도 기억이 안 난다고 하고. 그나저나 너라도 기별을 하지 그랬어. 너희 영감 소식을 어제야 들었다."

너도 기억을 못 한다는 말을, 할까 말까 망설이다 기어이 입에 담은 그 말을, 사다꼬는 흘려듣는다.

"늙으면 다 가는 것을 뭐하러 번거롭게……."

아이구, 너 잘났다, 소리를 그녀는 겨우 참는다. 사다꼬는 언제나 이런 식이다. 사소한 일에도 어쩔 줄 몰라 발을 동동 구르는 하루꼬와 달리 사다꼬는 어떤 일에도 흔들리지 않았다. 생각해보면 사다꼬의 인생은 동창들 중에서도 유독 굴곡이 많았다. 동경제대 나온 사다꼬의 남편은 혼인한 지 몇 달 지나지도 않아 산사람이 되었다. 그 남편을 따라 사다꼬도 산으로 갔고 근 10년 연락이 끊겼다. 산에서 남편을 잃은 사다꼬는 감옥살이를 마치고 고향으로 돌아왔다. 십수 년 뒤에 사다꼬는 저와 똑같은 이력을 가진 가난뱅이와 재혼을 했고, 사다

ko in the pharmacy the next market day, Sadako spun sharply, looking furtively at the line of customers waiting on the wooden chairs behind them.

"Keep that to yourself," she said. "That kind of gossip might leave Haruko on the edge, maybe even suicidal, who knows!"

Aiko was deeply hurt. She realized that Sadako knew already. There were no secrets between Haruko and Sadako.

All the more so then did Aiko push herself to help Haruko. Though Haruko was distant—glad when Aiko visited, indifferent when they said goodbye—she began to change after her husband's death. Haruko the widow became completely dependent on Aiko and her mind went completely blank in regards to Sadako.

"Haruko's really off the beam. She could soon follow her husband. Today she says she was late at my place because her man ate late. Said she couldn't remember you either. But you could have notified us about your husband. I only heard the news yesterday."

Sadako ignored Aiko's reference to Haruko's blankness about her, which had been said with difficulty after a few failed attempts.

꼬에 대해 늘 뭔가 석연치 않은 가슴앓이를 하던 그녀
는 당시로는 제법 거액이던 1,000원을 부조할 만큼 여
유가 생겼다. 공부 잘했다고 인생 잘 풀리는 게 아니다.
이래서 세상은 살아봐야 하는 거라고, 결혼식도 올리지
않은 채 들고나는 단칸방에 살림을 차린 사다꼬네 집에
갔던 그녀는 고개를 주억거리며 그제야 마음으로 받아
들인 친구의 등을 두드렸다. 사다꼬와 재혼한 가난뱅이
는 가난뱅이로도 모자라 읍내를 떠들썩하게 했던 재조
직사건에 걸려 10년 넘게 감옥살이를 했다. 간혹 사다
꼬는 병색 깊은 파리한 얼굴로 그녀가 운영하는 약방에
들러 소다를 찾았다. 위장약 하나 변변히 지어먹을 형
편도 안 되는 주제에 자존심은 제 낯빛보다 더 시퍼레
서 사다꼬는 기어이 몇 푼 되지 않는 약값을 카운터에
올려놓고 종종걸음으로 사라졌다. 그게 벌써 언제적 이
야긴가. 약사 면허도 없이 일본인이 물려주고 간 김약
방을 운영하던 시절이었다. 면허는 없어도 워낙 수완이
좋아 김약방은 일본인이 운영하던 시절보다 더 유명했
다. 특히 그녀가 한의사에게 의뢰해서 만든 고약과 피
부병 약이 효험이 있다고 소문이 나 옆 도시에서까지
손님이 몰려들었다. 이 바닥 돈은 김약방이 다 쓸어 담

"Death takes everyone in old age, why make a fuss about..."

Aiko barely restrained herself from saying, "Wow, aren't you noble!"

Vintage Sadako. Nothing fazed her, unlike Haruko who stamped her feet in frustration at life's smallest turn. In hindsight, of all their classmates, Sadako had had the most up and down life. She married the TIU man and within a few months he was a partisan in the mountains. Sadako followed him there and was incommunicado for about ten years. She lost her husband in the mountains, did a spell in prison herself, and then finally returned home.

Many years later, Sadako re-married; the man's background was similar to her own, and he was also a pauper. Aiko, who always felt a niggling soreness toward Sadako, got a boost with a well-wishing handout of a thousand won—big money in those times. Educational prowess didn't solve life's problems: You had to learn to put up with the world.

Aiko visited Sadako and her partner when they were living in their tiny one-room. They were not legally married. She remembered feeling then that she had put one over on Sadako. The man Sadako

는다는 소문이 자자할 정도였다. 그 돈으로 여러 사람 살판이 났다. 60년대 초반, 십수 년 교사생활을 했다면서 모아놓은 돈도 없이 하루꼬네가 고향으로 돌아왔을 때 떡하니 책방을 차려준 것도 그녀였다. 물론 10년에 걸쳐 하루꼬가 다 갚기는 했지만. 하루꼬에게 그 돈 갚으라는 말을 하지는 않았다. 애당초 줄 작정이었다. 주변머리 없는 하루꼬가 은행 이자 쳐서 마지막 한 닢까지 똑 부러지게 갚았을 뿐이다. 그녀는 그게 외려 서운했다. 조금만 살갑게 굴었더라면 사다꼬에게도 먹고살 밑천쯤 마련해줄 형편이 되고도 남았다. 돈을 잘 벌기도 했지만 그녀는 돈을 쓰는 데도 인색하지 않았던 것이다. 그러나 사다꼬는 단 한 번도 힘든 내색을 하지 않았다. 힘든 내색은커녕 언젠가는 그녀에게 따끔한 훈계를 늘어놓기도 했다. 좁은 읍내에 그녀에 관한 소문이 파다하게 나돌 무렵이었다.

어린 그녀의 가슴을 설레게 하던 박 조수는 약방을 그녀에게 맡겨두고는 국궁이니 색소폰이니, 쓰잘 데 없는 데 미쳐 밖으로만 나돌았다. 야리야리 부끄럼 많고 다정하던 박 조수는 알고 보니 그녀에게만이 아니라 세상 아무 여자에게나 부끄럼 많고 다정했다. 결국 박 조

had taken up with, for all his impecunious circumstances, spent more than ten years behind bars again because of his involvement in another incident that had the area in uproar.

Occasionally, Sadako—her face a sickly deep purple—would drop into the pharmacy for sodium carbonate. Even though she couldn't afford to buy a bottle of the stomach remedy, self-respect won out over desperation. After leaving a few pennies on the counter, she'd rush out the door. Aiko had taken over Kim's pharmacy from the original Japanese owners. It was an unlicensed business, but she was so adept at the work that the pharmacy established a better reputation than in former times. Word spread that her ointment and skin prescriptions in particular, which were made under the auspices of an oriental medicine doctor, were the finest in the city; she packed in the customers from even the city nearby. Rumor had it that all the money in town flowed into Kim's pharmacy. With this money, Aiko was able to help many people.

In the early 60s, Aiko funded Haruko's husband in setting up a bookstore. Haruko had come home in pitiful circumstances after more than ten years of his teaching: she had no savings. Sure, Haruko paid

수는 마흔도 되기 전에 첩년의 무르팍을 베고 자다 급사했다. 그 무렵엔 남편에 대한 정 따위는 흔적도 없이 사라져 쓸데없이 돈만 쓰고 속만 태우더니 시원코 잘됐다, 눈물도 나오지 않았다. 마지막으로 네가 듬뿍 사랑받았으니 보내는 길도 네가 알아서 하라고 첩년에게 돈뭉치만 던져놓고 그녀는 모르쇠로 일관했다. 아무리 그래도 본실이 너무하는 것 아니냐고 뒤에서 말들이 많은 모양이었지만 그녀는 신경 쓰지 않았다.

막내가 서울에 있는 고등학교에 진학한 뒤 그녀는 읍내 고등학교 선생과 눈이 맞았다. 술을 마신 다음 날이면 어김없이 박카스를 사먹으러 오는 남자였다. 역사 선생이었던 그 남자는 손가락이 유난히 길고 하앴다. 박 조수의 손도 그랬다는 것을 까맣게 잊고 그녀는 남자에게 흠뻑 빠졌다. 남자가 혼잣몸이었으면 자식들이야 뭐라던 재혼을 했으리라. 애석하게도 남자는 유부남이었고 결혼 직후부터 아내와 사이가 좋지 않았지만 우유부단하여 조강지처를 버릴 위인이 아니었다. 어쩔 수 없이 체념했으나 남자는 하루에도 몇 번씩 박카스를 사러 약방에 들렀다. 박카스를 건네주다 손이 스쳤을 때 전기에 감전이라도 된 듯 온몸이 저르르 떨렸다. 그 떨

Aiko over the next ten years, but Aiko never asked her to repay the debt. The money was a gift, but the inflexible Haruko wanted to pay back every penny, including interest, which saddened Aiko intensely. Aiko would have helped Sadako too, had Sadako given any hint of difficulty. Aiko had more than enough to fund her too. She had made a lot of money and she wasn't stingy. But Sadako never manifested any hardships to her. On the contrary, Sadako continued acting like Aiko's sharpest advisor.

In such a small town, stories spread about Aiko. Park, the pharmacy assistant who had won her heart, left her with the business while he took to the high life—archery and the saxophone. She found out after their marriage ended that he was indeed very affectionate, not only to her, but to every woman he ever met. Embarrassments abounded. He died suddenly before he turned forty, asleep with his head on his mistress' knee. At the time of his death all trace of Aiko's love for him had gone out of her. She failed to shed even a single tear. He had broken her heart – and was a useless spendthrift besides. Later, she was relieved. She sent a wad of money to his mistress: *You had all*

림을 예민한 남자는 놓치지 않았다. 남자가 길고 섬세한 손으로 덥석 그녀의 손을 움켜쥐었고 온몸에 힘이 빠져 그녀는 그만 스르르 주저앉고 말았다. 여름이었다. 그길로 두 사람은 택시를 불러 타고 옆 도시로 달려 갔다. 가는 내내 남자는 그녀의 손을 놓지 않았다. 손바닥이 흠뻑 젖었다. 손이 젖는 만큼 몸이 달아올랐다. 여관방에 들어서자마자 두 사람은 뱀처럼 뒤엉켰다. 남편과도 나눠보지 못한 뜨거운 정사였다. 남의 눈을 피한다고 피했지만 워낙 손바닥만 한 좁은 동네라 머지않아 두 사람의 정분을 알 만한 사람은 다 알게 되었다. 낯이 뜨겁기는 했다. 그러나 제 몸의 욕망을 죽이며 살고 싶지는 않았다. 남편은 죽었고 아직 젊은 그녀는 싱싱하게 살아 있었다.

그 무렵 사다꼬가 그녀를 찾아왔다. 소다만 사서 돌아가던 사다꼬가 웬일로 약방문을 닫을 때까지 돌아가지 않았다. 문을 닫은 뒤 사다꼬는 그녀를 똑바로 바라보았다. 질책하는 눈빛이었고 순간 그녀는 사다꼬가 소문을 알고 있음을 직감했다. 사다꼬답게 말은 짧고 직설적이었다.

"너는 여자이기 전에 어미야. 자식에게 부끄러운 짓은

his love; bury him. Out of earshot, many people said as a wife she had gone too far, but she didn't care.

After her youngest child made it to high school in Seoul, Aiko took up with a teacher in the local high school. He liked dropping in for a pick me up after a day binge-drinking. He was a history teacher and his fingers were uncommonly long and white. She fell head over heels for him, completely forgetting that assistant Park had similar hands. If he'd been single, she might have remarried, despite anything her children might say. Unfortunately, he was married, and though his relationship with his wife was cool from the beginning, he was too indecisive to divorce her. Aiko tried to distance herself from him, but he dropped in several times daily for a tonic. When their hands brushed in an exchange of goods, a jolt of electricity blazed through her.

The man persisted, aware of the effect he was having on her. He grasped her hand abruptly in his long, delicate one. She lost all feeling, all resistance. It was summer. They called a taxi and took off to a nearby city. All the way there, he didn't let go of her hand. Her palms were balls of sweat, as were her hands and her body. As soon as they got to the motel room, they entwined snake-like. This

말아야지. 사람이 어찌 욕망대로만 살겠니? 남자가 그리우면 책을 읽든지 공부를 하든지……."

말이 끝나기도 전에 그녀는 부들부들 떨면서 사다꼬의 뺨을 후려쳤다. 부들부들 떤 것이 수치심 탓이었는지 배신감 탓이었는지는 알 수 없다.

"재혼한 년이나 바람핀 년이나 뭐가 달라서!"

사다꼬는 뺨에 붉은 손자국을 품은 채 말갛게 그녀를 바라보다 아무 말 없이 돌아섰다. 알고 있었다. 뒤에서들 뭐라고 수군거리는지. 면전에서 쓴소리한 사다꼬야말로 친구라는 것도. 그래도 그 순간 그녀는 사다꼬의 잘난 척을 견딜 수 없었다. 어쩌면 사다꼬의 말이 그녀의 가장 아픈 곳을 건드린 것인지도 몰랐다. 아니, 그녀는 자식을 위해 최선을 다했다. 열심히 돈을 벌었고, 그 시절에 미국 유학도 보냈다. 어미로서 할 수 있는 일은 다했다. 아이들이 서울로 진학을 하면 만사 젖혀두고 따라가서 직접 집을 구했고, 믿을 만한 식모를 구하기 위해 사방으로 다리를 놓아 알아보았다. 아무리 평판이 좋아도 집에서 두어 해 지켜본 사람이 아니면 절대 아이들을 맡기지 않았다. 아이들 좋아하는 참게장을 직접 담갔고, 겨울이면 갓김치에 석박지에 고들빼기에 종류

44

was a flaming passion she had not experienced with her husband. They tried to avoid prying eyes but in a town no bigger than the palm of a hand, before long those who mattered knew of their tryst. She was overcome with embarrassment, but she had no desire to quell her body's sexual longings. Her husband was dead, but she was young and wonderfully alive.

Sadako came to see her. She bought the usual stomach powder but hung around until closing time. When all the customers had left, Sadako fixed her with a reproachful look. Aiko realized that Sadako had heard the rumors. What Sadako said was typical of her, short and to the point.

"You're a woman—but you're a mother first. Don't embarrass your children. Are you the slave of your sexual urges? If you feel like you need a man, go read or study..."

Before Sadako could finish, Aiko flushed violently and slapped her. Whether from betrayal or shame, who could say?

"What's the difference between a loose woman and a remarried bitch?"

Her cheek smarting, Sadako stared at Aiko without anger and turned away silently. Aiko knew that

도 다양하게 김장을 해서 보냈다. 그녀의 인생 10분의 9
는 아이들 것이었다. 나머지 1 정도는 나의 즐거움을 위
해 쓸 수도 있는 것 아닌가. 사다꼬를 보낸 뒤 그녀는 요
위에 엎어져 펑펑 울었다. 울면서도 그녀는 남자의 팔
베개가 그리웠고 살냄새가 그리웠다. 남자의 아내에게
결국 들통이 나 관계가 깨진 후에도 그녀는 사다꼬 보
란 듯이 남자를 만났다. 누가 뭐라던 사람답게 살고
싶었을 뿐이다. 지금도 그녀는 지난 세월을 후회하지
않는다. 그런데도 사다꼬만 보면 그날의 수치심이 되살
아난다.

사다꼬가 우유를 내온다. 따뜻하게 데운 우유다. 사다
꼬가 따뜻한 잔을 하루꼬의 손에 쥐어준다. 봄볕이 찬
란했으나 난방을 하지 않은 실내는 소름이 돋도록 서늘
하다.

"하루꼬, 나 감옥에서 나왔을 때 네가 만들어준 이 콩
물을 먹고 병을 고쳤잖아. 지금도 어디만 안 좋으면 콩
물을 먹는다. 내 만병통치약이야. 어여 마셔."

그 말에 그녀는 또 비위가 상한다. 김치며 토하젓이며
송이버섯이며 하루꼬에게 철철이 음식을 댄 것은 그녀
였다. 그녀는 하루꼬의 콩물 같은 건 먹어보지 못했다.

people were speaking ill of her behind her back and that Sadako was advising her as a real friend. But in that moment she couldn't bear Sadako's presumption. Sadako's words had probably found her most vulnerable spot. Hadn't she done her best for her children? She worked hard putting money together and sent one to study in America. She had done all a mother could do. When the children went to school in Seoul, she put everything to one side, personally found them a house, and searched everywhere until she found them a trustworthy maid. She would not entrust her children to just anyone, however good the references. She boxed crab marinated in soy sauce, which the children loved, and sent them all varieties of *kimchi* during the winter—leaf mustard *kimchi*; large diced radish *kimchi*; and lettuce *kimchi*. Her life was ninety percent for her children; was the remaining ten percent not hers to enjoy?

After Aiko sent Sadako off, she threw herself down on her sleeping mat and wept bitterly. She would have liked to pillow her head on the man's arm. She desired his scent. The relationship ended when his wife found out about it. Still, Aiko had shown Sadako that she could still win a man.

서점 한다고 늘 바쁘던 애가 콩 삶고 갈고 거르는 그 귀찮은 일을 마다하지 않았단 말이지, 믹서도 없던 그 시절에. 흐트러진 마음이 얼굴에 고스란히 드러난다. 픽, 사다꼬의 입에서 웃음이 새나온다.

"또 시작이다. 할망구가 되어서도 어쩌면 에이꼬는 보통학교 때랑 똑같니?"

"그러게 말이야. 너희 집엔 그 비싼 우유가 썩어났잖아. 그 우유, 사다꼬에게 주자는 말이 차마 안 나와서 콩물을 만들었구만."

드디어 기억의 실마리가 풀린 모양이다. 얼마만인지 웃으며 말을 받는 하루꼬가 반갑고, 반갑지 않다.

"너 괜찮은 거야?"

"내가 괜찮지 그럼."

"영감 죽은 것은 알아?"

"얘가 지금 무슨 소리를 하는 거야?"

하루꼬가 아무것도 모르는 얼굴로 되묻는다. 영감이 아침밥 먹기 싫다고 했다는 말을 그녀는 차마 하지 못한다. 이렇게라도 돌아왔으니 다행이다. 이게 다 사다꼬 덕이라는 데 생각이 미치자 그녀는 그새 하루꼬 정신 돌아온 반가움을 잊고 아이처럼 불퉁거린다.

Let people say what they like, Aiko just wanted to live like a human being. Even now, she had no regrets about the past, but the sight of Sadako was enough to bring back the shameful memory of that day.

Sadako brought out milk. She put a warm glass in Haruko's hand. The spring light was shining in, but they shivered in the unheated room.

"Haruko, when I got out of jail, you cured me with your boiled bean mixture. I still take it when I'm not feeling well. It's the elixir for all my aches. Please, drink."

Aiko sniffed. She was the one who had brought Haruko *kimchi*, salted baby shrimp and pine mushrooms year round. But she had never tasted Haruko's bean brew. How could Haruko, supposedly so busy with the bookstore, have had all that time for boiling, mashing and brewing beans. There were no electric mixers then, either. Aiko's feelings were written all over her face. Sadako laughed, a hiss of breath escaping.

"She's at it again. An ugly old bag now, how can Aiko be the same as she was back in our school days?" Sadako mused to Haruko.

"You're right. Remember when that expensive

"너한테 콩물은커녕 따뜻한 숭늉 한 그릇 못 얻어먹었다."

쯧쯧, 하루꼬가 혀를 찬다.

"아이구, 네가 내 고추장 맛있대서 고추장, 된장, 간장, 너희 애들 셋이 다 커서 시집장가 갈 때까지 내가 다 댔다. 영감하고 나하고 먹은 것보다 너희 집으로 간 게 몇 배였어. 너희 애들, 다 너 닮아 뱃구레가 크잖아. 그뿐이야? 너희 애들이 내가 만든 딸기잼 한 번 먹더니 환장을 해서 그것도 평생 댔고. 조목조목 읊어보랴? 내가 해줄 건 그런 것밖에 없어서 할 수 있는 건 다 했구만 또 심통이다. 아무튼 에이꼬 심통은 알아줘야 해."

하루꼬 말이 사실은 사실이었다. 시집간 지금도 딸애는 하루꼬의 된장을 찾았다. 그러고 보니 하루꼬 남편이 죽기 전까지는 딸애가 하루꼬 된장을 먹었다. 할 말은 없었지만 뭔지 모르게 입맛이 썼다. 생각해보면 그거야 준 만큼 돌려받은 것이다. 빚지고는 못 사는 성격이라 빚을 갚듯 하루꼬는 장을 담갔을 것이다. 아무것도 주지 않은 사다꼬가 얻어먹은 콩물은 빚이 아니라 마음이었다.

"그 욕심으로 이만큼 산 거지, 뭐."

milk curdled in your house, and I couldn't suggest giving it to Sadako. I made soya milk instead."

Finally, the thread of memory was unraveling. Haruko hadn't laughed or conversed for some time. Aiko was both glad and not.

"Are you all right?"

"Of course, I'm all right."

"Do you know your husband is dead?"

"What are you saying?" Haruko looked as if she didn't understand the question.

Aiko didn't remind Haruko that she had said her husband had had no appetite this morning. The return to normalcy was good. And this was all thanks to Sadako, Aiko realized. Aiko lost her newfound joy about Haruko and pouted like a child again.

"I never got a cup of hot rice tea, not to mention bean brew from you," Aiko finally blurted.

Haruko clucked her tongue loudly. "My, you said you liked my pepper paste, so I kept your three children filled with pepper paste, soy sauce and soy bean paste until they got married. What I sent your house topped everything that my husband and I ate combined. They guzzled their fill as much as you. What's more, once your girls tasted my strawberry jam they were wild about it and I fed

사다꼬가 또 잘난 척을 하고 나선다. 그 지난한 세월
도 잘난 척을 꺾지는 못한 모양이다. 여든이 넘었는데
도 사다꼬의 말에 비위가 상하는 그녀 역시 변한 게 없
다. 그녀는 욕심도 많고 지기 싫어하는 성품이라 그렇
고, 사다꼬는 책이든 제 자신이든 한 치 흐트러짐 없이
반듯하게 줄 서 있어야 직성이 풀리게 생겨먹어 그렇
다. 그런 걸 알면서도 번번이 비위가 상한다. 알면서도
어쩌지 못하는 것이 성품이다. 언제 상을 당했냐는 듯
말로야 초연하지만 사다꼬의 안색은 초췌하다 못해 병
색이 완연하다. 원래 입도 짧은 데다 큰일을 겪었으니
제대로 먹지도 못했을 것이다.

"밥이나 제대로 먹는 거야?"

"그럼. 하루 세 끼 꼬박꼬박 챙겨먹고 있어. 뭐하자고
이렇게 챙겨먹나 싶다가도 내 몸 건사 잘하는 게 자식
에게 해줄 수 있는 유일한 선물이다 싶어서 약 먹듯이
먹는다."

"어련하시겠어."

기어이 그녀의 입에서 비아냥이 나오고 만다. 세월은
정작 둥글려야 할 것은 그냥 놔두고 육신만 갉아먹는
모양이다. 사다꼬는 저를 쥐 잡듯 잡아 군기 바짝 든 신

them that too. I could go on; this was all I could do, but I did them all. And now, Aiko, you're cross; admit it."

Haruko was right. Aiko's married daughter still looked for Haruko's soybean paste. Actually, she had eaten Haruko's bean paste until Haruko's husband died.

Aiko had nothing against Haruko but somehow the whole thing left a bitter taste. Really, Aiko had received as much as she had given. With her disposition for not wanting to live in debt, Haruko had settled debt considerations between them by giving so. The bean brew that Sadako had received— even though Sadako never gave Haruko anything— was not a debt, but a gift from the heart.

"Her greed's kept her alive," Sadako said in her lofty, superior fashion. Days of hardship hadn't broken down old habits, and being over eighty hadn't changed Aiko's vexation at Sadako's words either. Aiko had greed in plenty and a personality that hated to lose. That was true; Sadako gloried in standing tall and refusing to budge an inch, either on her opinion on books or on herself. That also was true.

Despite being able to acknowledge these differ-

병처럼 모진 세월을 견딘다. 그것이 사다꼬의 방식임을 알면서도 늘그막까지 무어 그리 안간힘을 쓰는지 그녀는 안쓰럽다 못해 짜증스럽다. 기대어 견디는 법을 사다꼬는 알지 못한다. 40년을 함께 산 남편에게도 아마 기대보지 못했을 것이다. 그러니 저렇듯 초연하게 버텨낼 수 있는 건지도 모른다.

"너는 좋겠다. 자식이 있어서. 나도 자식이 있었으면 이럴 때 힘이 됐을 텐데."

반짝 생기가 돌았던 하루꼬가 다시 풀이 죽는다. 그녀가 위로의 말을 꺼내려는 찰나 사다꼬가 먼저 말을 받는다.

"그럴 거 없어. 그게 다 짐이야. 없었던 듯이 깨끗하게 가면 그게 젤이지. 물려줄 재산도 없고 몸고생 마음고생만 시키다가 부모 가는 뒤치다꺼리까지 시키려니, 그게 고민이다, 요새 내가."

"그래도 너는 의지할 데가 있잖아. 의지할 자식도 없으니 나부터 보내놓고 자기가 뒤따라가겠다고 해놓고는……."

하루꼬의 눈에 그렁그렁 눈물이 맺힌다. 그러겠노라 굳게 약속했던 하루꼬의 남편은 늘 그랬듯 하루꼬에게

ences, Aiko clearly felt aggrieved. Knowing, but still being at a loss was a large part of her personality. Sadako was aloof as to be almost impervious to pain, yet her pale face clearly showed the evidence of her poor health. She had never had a big appetite. This plus her husband's death interfered with her eating properly.

"Are you eating normally?"

"Sure, three meals a day as a rule. It's not what I always want, but staying healthy is the only gift I can give to my child, so I eat as if the food's been prescribed to me."

"Exactly!"

Aiko couldn't withhold her sarcasm. Age had failed to broaden her mind; it had only succeeded in making her old and weak. Sadako had held onto her life by the teeth—a novice soldier with gun always at the ready. Aiko knew this was Sadako's style, but it annoyed her that she still wasn't strong enough to accept it. Sadako had no concept of leaning on someone and toughing it out together. In forty years of marriage, she'd probably never relied on her husband even once. That was why she was now coolly toughing it out to the end.

"It's well for you two, though. You have kids. If I

팔베개를 해주고 자다가 세상을 떠났다. 죽은 남편에게 안긴 채 잠에서 깨어난 하루꼬는 그대로 혼절을 했다. 두 사람을 발견한 것은 하도 전화를 받지 않기에 무슨 일인가 싶어 찾아간 그녀였다. 그녀는 하루꼬가 남편의 품에 안겨 잠을 자는 줄 알았다. 하루꼬는 평생을 저렇게 한 남자의 품에 안겨 살았구나, 부러운 마음에 발소리를 죽여 돌아 나오려는 찰나, 이미 정오가 가깝다는 데 생각이 미쳤고, 흔들어보니 하루꼬는 깨어났으나 그 남편은 이미 딱딱하게 굳어 깨어나지 않았다.

"너는 평생 남편에게 의지하고 살았잖아. 둘이서 깨가 쏟아지게. 나는 단 한 시간도 그런 세월을 못 살아봤다."

사다꼬도 그게 부러웠구나. 어쩐지 그녀는 그런 사다꼬가 가깝게 느껴진다. 언제였는지, 갓 구운 카스텔라를 들고 서점에 간 적이 있다. 학생들 등하교 시간이나 되어야 손님이 드는 서점은 고즈넉했다. 그렇게 자주 봐도 영 말이 없는 하루꼬 남편이 불편해서 그녀는 창 밖에서 서점 안을 기웃거렸다. 참고서를 들이는 참인지 두 사람은 책 뭉치를 풀고 있었다. 하루꼬의 앞머리가 흘러내리자 남편이 장갑을 벗고는 천천히 쓸어 올렸다. 머리카락을 한올 한올 정성스럽게 귀 뒤로 넘긴 남편은

had kids, they'd be my strength in the bad times."

Haruko, alive again for a moment, just as quickly lost heart again. Sadako answered before Aiko could interject words of comfort.

"That's not true. Everything's a burden. Better to leave the world as if you'd never been here. I've no fortune to give to anyone. I don't want my son to worry about having to take care of me. Besides, he'll have to look after my funeral. That's my great concern these days."

"But you have someone for support. My husband said he wanted to survive me because we had no child to lean on. But..."

Tears filled Haruko's eyes. Her husband hadn't been able to keep his promise to look after her. He let her pillow her head on his arm and died. She awoke in his dead embrace and promptly fainted.

That was the way that Aiko found them. She'd been thinking it strange that they hadn't answered the phone. Even then, she'd thought that Haruko was asleep in her husband's embrace. She envied her that life-long place in the bosom of one man. About to return home without further ado, she suddenly averted to it being already noon. When she shook them, only Haruko came to—the man,

몇 번이고 하루꼬의 뺨을 쓰다듬었다. 다정하고 정성스러운 손길이었다. 하루꼬가 부끄러운 듯 배시시 웃었다. 그 웃음 또한 다정하고 따뜻했다. 단 한 시간도 그런 세월을 살아보지 못했노라는 사다꼬의 말을 그녀는 속속들이 이해할 수 있을 것 같다. 댓 명의 남자를 거쳐 왔으나 떠날 것을 알고 있던 남자들의 손길은 뜨겁기는 했어도 정성스럽지는 않았다. 그녀가 죽고 못 살아 결혼까지 하게 됐던 남편도 자꾸 엉겨 붙는 그녀를 밀어내기만 했다. 그러다가 결국 다른 여자의 품으로 달아나버렸다. 돈도 자식도 다 제 맘대로 됐으나 남자만큼은 단 한 번도 제 맘대로 되지 않았다.

"못 살아보기는? 네 남편이 너 대신 장 다 보고 했잖아?"

"장이야 봐줬지. 내가 몸이 아파 못 다니니까. 그것뿐이야. 둘이 머리 맞대고 앉아 다정한 얘기 한 번 해본 적이 없는데 뭘."

"그럼 무슨 이야기를 했는데?"

그녀 앞에서는 울기만 하던 하루꼬가 웬일로 눈물 그렁그렁한 채 통곡은 하지 않고 따박따박 말을 받는다.

"무슨 이야기는 무슨 이야기. 빨갱이들이 무슨 이야기

58

pitifully cold, did not awaken.

"All your life you had your man for support. Like peas in a pod. I never had an hour of that."

Ah, even Sadako was envious. Aiko warmed to this Sadako.

Aiko once went to the bookstore with a sponge cake. There were fewer customers during school hours, so the store was calm and quiet. She checked at the window first because, as often as she had met Haruko's husband, he had remained a man of few words. He still made her uncomfortable.

The pair were opening a bundle of books, probably reference books or such. When Haruko's hair fell down over her forehead, her husband took off his gloves and pushed it back slowly. He curled her hair back gracefully, strand by strand, over her ears, and then he patted her cheek repeatedly— tender, loving strokes. Haruko laughed shyly, but her smile was also tender and warm.

Aiko immediately understood that Sadako had not experienced an hour of that kind of intimacy. A few men had come Aiko's way, but their touch, however warming, was always insincere. It was the kind of touch of someone who knew they'd be leaving

59

를 했겠어? 남몰래 소곤소곤 사상 이야기나 했겠지. 그
러려고 빨갱이랑 결혼한 것 아냐?"

그녀가 냉큼 말을 받았고, 사다꼬가 웃으며 고개를 끄
덕인다. 감옥에서 나온 뒤 사다꼬에게 집적거리는 남자
가 한둘이 아니었다. 그중에는 의사도 있고 검사도 있
었다. 사다꼬가 잡혔을 때 취조했다는 검사는 멀리 떨
어진 이곳까지 몇 번이나 사다꼬를 만나러 왔다. 그런
사람들 다 뿌리치고 왜 하필 가난한 빨갱이냐고 물었더
니 사다꼬는 그래야 속엣말이라도 하고 살지, 씁쓸하게
웃었다.

"너는 대체 무슨 맛으로 살았니?"

오래전에 궁금했던 것을 그녀는 이제야 묻는다. 돈도
없고 남편도 보잘 것 없고 직업도 없고 있는 거라곤 딸
랑 아들 하나—어릴 때야 공부를 곧잘 했지만 지금은
겨우 출판사나 다니며 셋방살이를 면하지 못한—뿐인
사다꼬가 평생 누구에게도 기죽지 않고 당당한 이유를
그녀는 좀처럼 이해할 수 없었다.

"너야 자식 때문에 살았을 거고, 하루꼬는 남편 때문
에 살았을 거고, 글쎄, 나는 뭣 땜에 살았나……."

"사다꼬는 사상이 있잖아, 사상이. 우리 영감도 그랬

soon. The man she loved and married turned her away when she needed his warm touch. In the end he went off to the arms of another. Aiko had her way with money and kids but no satisfaction whatsoever in the way of men.

"No life together? Didn't your man go to the market for you?"

"Yes, when he was in the mood. I was too sick to go. That's only part of it. We never sat down for a heart-to-heart talk."

"So, what did you talk about?"

Haruko only cried in Aiko's company. Now, however, though tears still filled her eyes, she questioned Sadako in a calm, crank-free way.

"What did they talk about? What do any communists talk about? That's why Sadako married a communist, so she could whisper their shared secret ideology," Aiko quickly interjected.

Sadako smiled and nodded her head.

When Sadako was released from prison, several men were already waiting for her at her house, a doctor and a prosecutor among them. And her interrogator in jail made the long trip to her house several times. They kept pestering her about why she had taken a commie husband. Laughing bitter-

는걸. 어쩌면 우리 영감은 나보다 그게 더 중요했는지도 몰라."

"네 남편이 사다꼬 같은 빨갱이였다고? 정말? 그걸 왜 말 안 했어?"

"세상이 금한 걸 말해 뭣해? 그리고 그런 생각을 가졌달 뿐 평생 책이나 팔다 갔는데 뭘. 그런데도 그 생각은 평생 떨치질 못하더라. 사상이 대체 뭔지……."

그녀는 까맣게 몰랐다. 놀라지 않는 걸 보니 아마 사다꼬는 진작 알고 있었던 모양이다. 이 두 사람은 번번이 뒤통수를 친다. 어쩌면 아직도 그녀가 모르는 뭔가가 있을지 모른다.

"사상이고 뭐고, 살아보니 다 덧없다. 죽으면 다 한 줌 재지, 뭐."

말은 그렇게 하지만 거실을 가득 메우고 있는 책장에는 순 그런 책들뿐이다. 지금도 사다꼬의 곁에는 《통일광장》이라는 잡지인지 책인지가 놓여 있다.

"영감 죽고 나니 그러네. 더 살아 무슨 영화를 볼 것도 아니고 할 수만 있다면 혀 깨물고 깨끗이 죽었으면 좋겠구만……. 내 한 몸이면 정말 그러겠어."

사다꼬는 그러기로 작정하면 정말 그러고도 남을 위

ly, Sadako rejoined: I thought I could at least open my heart to the man.

"What in the world do you live for?" Aiko said.

That was a question she had been pondering a long time: Sadako had no money; she'd had a useless husband, no job, and just one son—an excellent student though now trifling with book publishing and living in a rented room—but she was never discouraged by anyone in her long life. For the life of her, Aiko couldn't understand this.

"You lived for your kids. Haruko lived for her husband. Me, who knows what I lived for?"

"You're an ideologue, Sadako. My husband was into ideology, too. Maybe he thought ideology was more important than me."

"Your husband was a Red like Sadako? Really? Why didn't you ever say so?"

"Why talk about something forbidden? And he only entertained the thought. His whole life was the bookstore, but he never shook off those thoughts, never. What's ideology, anyway?"

Aiko was at a loss. Sadako's lack of surprise was a sign that she had known about Haruko's husband. Those two occasionally gave her a pounding headache. There still were other things she didn't know.

인이다. 그러지 못하는 것은 그런 죽음이 혹 자식에게 상처가 될까 싶은 어미로서의 염려 때문일 것이다. 남자에게 달려가고 싶은 그녀의 마음을 막은 것은 오직 하나, 치마폭을 붙잡는 자식의 손길이었다. 아이들이 큰 뒤로야 거침없이 달려갔지만.

"나도 몇 번이고 죽으려고 했는데 그게, 나는 사다꼬 같지 않아서, 영감 따라가고 싶은 마음은 굴뚝같은데 나는 죽었다 깨나도 내 손으로 죽지는 못하겠어."

"죽긴 왜 죽어! 하루라도 더 재미나게 살아야지."

그녀는 괜스레 버럭 소리를 지른다. 노인네 죽고 싶다는 말은 처녀 시집가기 싫다는 말과 더불어 3대 거짓말 중의 하나라는데, 하루꼬와 사다꼬는 시집가기 싫다는 말도 거짓말이 아니었다. 늙은 지금 이것들이 죽고 싶다는 말 또한 거짓이 아닐지 모른다. 그러나 그녀는 두 사람과 달리 죽음이 두렵다. 아직은 가고 싶지 않다. 대체 뭐가 다른 걸까? 그것을 열넷에도 몰랐고 여든둘인 지금도 그녀는 알지 못한다.

"갈 테면 너희들이나 가라. 나는 천년만년 살라니까."

하루꼬와 사다꼬가 시선을 마주치며 웃음을 터뜨린다. 하루꼬의 웃음을 참으로 오랜만에 본다. 하루꼬도

"Ideology? In the end, life just whips past you. You die, and what's left but a handful of ashes," Sadako said. The books lining all the shelves of her room were all related to ideology. A journal called "Unification Plaza" lay open beside Sadako.

"After my husband died, I had no desire to live for some impossible imaginary future. I'd prefer to clench my teeth and go along cleanly if possible. If I were alone, that's the way I'd want it."

If Sadako set it up, she would well be able to do it. The only downside to this was a mother's fear of the injury that a death like this could inflict on her son. The only thing holding Aiko back from running to a man was her children's grip on her skirts. With the children grown, she would run without a moment's hesitation.

"I wanted to die a few times," Haruko said. "I'm not like Sadako. Though I've a burning need to follow my man, I couldn't do it with my own hand."

"Why die? Even one more day being alive is precious!" Aiko said.

The old want to die and girls hate the day when they must marry: two of the three great lies. But when Haruko and Sadako said they hated getting married, they weren't. And when they now said that

그 사실을 의식했는지 머쓱하게 웃음을 거둔다. 그러나 잠시의 웃음은 소녀 시절처럼 해맑다.

"자주 좀 모이자. 영감도 없으니 나도 이제 놀러도 다니고 해야겠다."

웃음 끝에 사다꼬가 덧붙인다. 사다꼬는 지난 5년, 남편이 앓아누운 뒤로 아예 문밖출입도 하지 못했다.

"아이구, 언제는 사는 게 덧없다더니…….""

"에이꼬 네 말이 맞다. 죽지 못할 바에는 재미나게 살아야지."

사다꼬는 이렇게 불쑥 물러나서 사람 맥 빠지게 하는 데 도사다.

"나 배고파. 뭐 먹을 거 없어, 사다꼬?"

그녀가 산해진미를 올려도 먹는 둥 마는 둥 하던 하루꼬가 먹을 것을 찾는다. 하루꼬의 염장질은 이런 식이다.

"그래, 천년만년 살려면 일단 밥부터 먹어야지. 오랜만에 우리 밥이나 같이 먹자."

사다꼬가 일어서자 관절이 요란하게 투둑거린다. 과부 셋이 하하얗게 웃음을 터뜨린다. 열네 살의 사다꼬가 일어설 때도 저런 소리가 들렸다.

they wanted to die, this probably wasn't a lie either. But, Aiko, unlike them, was afraid of death. She didn't want to go yet. What was the difference between them? She didn't know at fourteen, and she didn't know at eighty-two either.

"Take off, you two, if you want. I want another ten thousand years."

Haruko and Sadako looked at each other and burst out laughing. This was a first for Haruko in a long time. And possibly that realization made her quickly stop laughing. However, that momentary burst of laughter echoed the bright trill of her youth.

"Let's get together more often. With my husband gone, I need to get out and about and enjoy myself more," Sadako said with a laugh. Sadako had been cut-off from the world for the five or six years that her husband was ill at home.

"Huh, you just said that life was meaningless..."

"Aiko, you're right. If we can't die, let's make the most of living," Sadako said, adept at giving way and wearing one down.

"I'm hungry, anything to eat here, Sadako?" Haruko said. She'd only pick at something delicate prepared by Aiko; now she was looking for food. That

"상 치른 집에 먹을 거나 있어?"

집에 가서 뭘 좀 가져올까 싶어 그녀가 몸을 일으키며 묻는다.

"누가 밑반찬을 좀 가져왔어."

주는 게 없는데도 사다꼬 주변에는 늘 사람이 많았다. 젊을 때는 제 아무리 날고 기던 사람이라도 늙어 돈 없으면 찾는 사람이 없다는데 아직도 사다꼬는 찾는 사람이 있는 모양이다.

"하루꼬, 아직도 두릅 좋아해?"

냉장고를 뒤지며 사다꼬가 묻는다.

"그럼. 식성이 어디 가나? 아직도 두릅이 있어?"

"누가 좀 갖다준 걸 영감 주려고 아껴놨었거든. 오래 먹이려고 조금씩만 줬는데 다 못 먹고 갔네."

잠시 말이 끊긴다. 어룽거리는 봄볕처럼 두 과부의 눈에 눈물이 어룽거린다. 그 눈물이 흘러내리기 전에 그녀가 얼른 묻는다.

"나 좋아하는 고기는 없어?"

"참, 에이꼬는 삼겹살 좋아하지? 여기 어디 얼려둔 게 있을 텐데……."

"치워라. 언제 죽을지 모르는데 돈 뒀다 뭘 해. 맛있는

was her way of stoking Aiko's anger.

"Okay, if we're going to live ten thousand years, we'd better start with eating. It's been a while, let's eat."

Sadako's joints cracked loudly when she got up. The three widows burst out laughing. Even at fourteen, Sadako's joints cracked.

"What's there to eat after a funeral?" Aiko thought, rising to go to her own place and bring back some food.

"Someone brought me a few savory side dishes," Sadako said. Though Sadako didn't give things to anyone, she always had a lot of people around her. It's said that one's assured pulling power in younger days does not guarantee people sticking around in old penniless days: Sadako still had people coming to see her, apparently.

"Haruko, do you still like new Japanese *fatsia shoots?*" Sadako said. She rooted around in her fridge.

"Of course. Your tastes never change! You still have some new shoots?"

"Someone gave them to me and I was saving them, sparing them so that my husband would have some for a long time, but he left most of them

생고기 사다 먹자. 오거리 봉성정육점 고기 맛있더라."

그녀는 급히 신발을 꿰찬다. 웬일로 사다꼬가 말리지
않는다. 가난하게 살던 젊은 시절, 사다꼬는 그녀가 고
기 한 근을 사준대도 마다했었다. 고맙고 이상해서 뒤
돌아봤더니 사다꼬와 하루꼬가 주방 탁자에 머리를 맞
대고 앉아 있다.

"야!"

어릴 때처럼 우렁찬 목소리로 그녀가 고함을 지른다.
사다꼬와 하루꼬가 무슨 일인가 싶어 그녀를 바라본다.

"나 없을 때 또 비밀 이야기 하면 죽어!"

그녀는 쾅, 요란하게 문을 닫는다. 아무리 엄포를 놓
아도 저것들은 또 그녀가 모르는 뭔가를 속닥일 것이
다. 어려서부터 그랬다. 시멘트로 포장된 빌라 주차장
에 거칠 데 없는 봄볕이 가득하다. 부신 눈을 함초롬히
뜬 채 그녀는 씩씩하게 걸음을 옮긴다. 앞으로 몇 년을
더 살까? 1년? 혹은 10년? 아직 그녀는 아픈 데 없이 건
강하다. 허리도 굽지 않았고 그 흔한 관절염도 없다. 그
래도 내일을 장담할 수 없는 나이이긴 하지만 그녀는
살아 있는 한 재미있게 살 작정이다. 살비듬 부스스 떨
어지는 노파지만 치근대는 대서소 김 영감도 있다. 김

behind."

Their conversation halted briefly. Like the shimmering spring sunlight, tears glistened in the eyes
of the two widows. Before the tears started to
flow, Aiko jumped in.

"Isn't there any meat for me? You know how I
like it."

"Ah, yes, Aiko likes pork belly, doesn't she? I
think there should be some frozen here some-
where."

"Leave it. Who knows when we'll die? What's the
use of saving money? Let's get some fresh meat.
Bong-Seong butcher's at the intersection has the
best."

Aiko quickly slipped on her shoes. Strangely, Sadako made no move to stop her. In her young,
poverty stricken days, Sadako would reject even a
half kilo of meat that Aiko might have bought for
her. Grateful, but also feeling a little strange, Aiko
turned around. Sadako and Haruko were already
head to head at the kitchen table.

"Hey!" she roared, in the booming voice of her
youth. Both looked at her in puzzlement.

"No secrets during my absence or I'll kill you
both!"

영감 팔베개를 베고 자다 죽는 것도 나쁘지 않겠다. 그
녀는 봄볕 속으로 네 활개를 치며 걸음을 옮긴다.

「숲의 대화」, 도서출판 은행나무, 2013

She closed the door with a resounding clang. Despite her warning, they would always get into matters that excluded her. It had always been that way. The cemented car park outside Sadako's place was filled with serene spring sunlight. Adjusting for a second to the dazzling light, Aiko moved off briskly. How long? A year? Ten? She was still healthy, without aches or pains. She was straight as an arrow and free of the usual arthritis. At her age there were no guarantees for tomorrow, but she was determined to live an interesting life for as long as she was around. She might be a scaly old hag but there were still a few men throwing looks her way: Kim, the notary man, for example. To die in her sleep, pillowed on Kim's arm, wouldn't be so bad. Hips swaying, Aiko walked into the spring light.

* This translation is included with permission from the newspaper *The Korea Times* where it was originally published on November 4, 2010.

Translated by Brendan MacHale and Kim Yoon-kyung

해설

Afterword

삶은 오래 지속된다

장성규 (문학평론가)

정지아는 현재 한국 문단에서 특별한 위상을 지니는
작가이다. 그녀는 해방 이후 남한 사회에서 금기시되었
던 '빨치산'들의 이야기를 다룬 『빨치산의 딸』로 작품 활
동을 시작하며 당대 변혁운동의 역사적 정체성을 확인
하는 문학적 성과를 거둔 바 있다. 주목되는 것은 변혁
운동의 전반적인 퇴조 이후 이른바 '후일담' 문학이 대
두하던 시기를 거쳐 정지아가 보여주는 문학적 모색의
밀도이다. 그녀는 과거의 도그마를 반복하지도 않으며,
동시에 섣부른 과거에 대한 '폐기'를 보여주지도 않는
다. 오히려 과거 민중문학의 내적 한계를 직시하며, 그
가운데서 충분히 조명되지 못한 소소한 삶의 결들을 '복

Life Endures

Jang Sung-kyu (literary critic)

Jeong Ji-a currently holds a special position among the Korean literary circle. She started her writing career with, *The Daughter of the Partisan*, which deals with guerilla warfare, a subject that had been taboo in South Korea since Korea's independence from Japan. This was a great literary achievement that re-evaluated the historical identity of the reform movements of those times, and was notable especially due to the density of the literary reflection Jeong demonstrated during a time when the so-called "backstory literature" had a wide readership after the waning of reform movements in general. She neither subscribes to the ideologies of the past nor dismisses it prematurely

원'시키는 것이 그녀의 문학적 문제의식이다.

이런 맥락에서「봄날 오후, 과부 셋」은 그 문제성이 도드라지는 작품이다. 얼핏 이 작품은 늙은 과부 셋의 일상을 다룬 소품으로 보인다. 그런데 정작 이들의 '과거'를 추적하면 그 무게가 만만치 않음을 알 수 있다. 남편과 함께 빨치산으로 활동하며 '사상'의 힘에 의탁했던 사다꼬, 4월 혁명을 전후하여 교원 운동에 참여했던 남편을 둔 하루꼬, 그리고 난봉꾼이었던 남편으로 인해 청춘을 보낸 에이꼬. 이들은 과거 민중문학의 흐름 속에서 자신의 삶을 증언할 기회를 '박탈'당했던 이들이다. 그러니까 중요했던 것은 어디까지나 동경제대 출신의 빨치산인 남편이나, 혹은 전주사범 출신의 남편이었던 셈이다. 이 과정에서 정작 끈질기게 삶을 직조해 온 이들의 삶은 주변적인 것으로 간주되었다.

그런 면에서 이 작품의 주인공인 에이꼬가 남편의 몫으로 환원되지 않는 자신만의 고유한 욕망을 실현하고 있다는 점은 중요하다. 그녀는 난봉꾼 남편의 죽음에 흔들리지 않은 채, 자신의 여성으로서의 욕망에 충실한 삶을 택한다. 생계의 위기에 처한 하루꼬 부부에게 책방을 내주는 것도 그녀이며, 사상의 무게에 눌린 사다

as stale. Rather, she identifies the internal limitations of past *minjung* literature, or the "people's literature," and makes it her task to "restore" the details of everyday life that may not have received the attention they deserved.

"Spring Afternoon, Three Widows" accomplishes just this. At a glance, this piece looks like a sketch of three old widows. However, we find considerable weight in the stories of their past. Sadako was a member of a partisan group along with her husband and relied on the power of ideology, Haruko's husband was part of the educators' movement following the April Revolution, and Aiko wasted her youth on a husband who was a womanizer. In the current of *minjung* literature, these characters had been robbed of the opportunity to relate their account of the past. While the Tokyo Imperial University-educated partisan husband or the Jeonju University Education School-alumnus husband took the spotlight, the wives' strenuous efforts to maintain a life was considered a mere backdrop.

In this sense, it is significant that Aiko, the protagonist of the story, fulfills her own desire, separate from her husband's. She chooses a life that is true to her female desires rather than being unrav-

꼬의 삶을 지탱해주는 것도 그녀이다. 에이꼬로 인해 비로소 남편들의 서사 대신 '과부'들의 서사가 가능해지는 셈이다. 그리고 이 서사가 어떠한 이데올로기보다도 오래 지속되는 삶의 무게를 지탱하고 있음은 물론이다.

어쩌면 한국 문학은 지나치게 형제·남편들의 연대에 집중해왔는지도 모른다. 이 과정에서 역으로 자매·과부들의 이야기는 부당하게 소거되어온 감이 있다. 이는 특히 일련의 민중문학적 경향의 작품에서 두드러지는 한계이기도 하다. 정지아의 이 작품이 중요한 것은 바로 이 때문이다. 그녀는 이데올로기를 담지한 형제·남편들의 이야기 대신, 삶을 담지한 자매·과부들의 이야기를 복원한다. 그리고 이를 통해 거대 담론으로부터 소거된 이들의 목소리를 복원하는 작업에 성공한다. 따라서 이 작품의 인물들이 모두 일제시대의 이름으로 호명되는 것은 필연적이다. 자매들의 연대가 발생한 기원이 그때이기 때문이며, 이는 민족주의 등의 이데올로기로 대체될 수 있는 성격의 것이 아니기 때문이다. 그렇게 정지아는 에이꼬와 하루꼬, 사다꼬의 삶을 직조하고 있다.

여전히 한국사회의 현실은 암담하며, 문학의 사회적

eled by the death of her womanizing husband. It is Aiko who offers the Haruko couple the bookstore when they are faced with a financial predicament, and supports Sadako as she struggles with a life overwhelmed by the weight of ideology. The narrative of the widows, not the husbands, is given voice through Aiko. And it goes without saying that their narrative carries the burden of life that far outlasts any ideology.

Perhaps Korean literature has thus far placed too much emphasis on the male narratives, unfairly suppressing the female narrative in the process. This is especially true in the *minjung* literature genre. Jeong Ji-a's work is especially important because it restores the female narrative that embodies everyday life rather than relating the male narrative that represents ideology, and in the process restores women's voices that had been silenced in the grand narrative. It is therefore also significant that the characters are all referred to by their Japanese names, because the Colonial Era served as the origins of the womens' solidarity that cannot be replaced with nationalistic ideologies. Jeong Ji-a observes the lives of Aiko, Haruko, and Sadako thus squarely.

역할 역시 중요하다. 그럼에도 불구하고 과거 민중문학의 한계를 내파하려는 문학적 모색은 절대적으로 부족한 감이 있다. 특히나 과거 민중문학의 유산을 손쉽게 '후일담'의 형식으로 소비하려는 경향은 결국 한국문학의 풍부한 자산을 매몰시킨다는 점에서 그 위험성이 크다. 반면 정지아는 자신의 작품 활동을 시작한 『빨치산의 딸』의 바로 그 자리에서 다시 시작한다. 그 자리에서 미처 말하지 못한 자매들의 서사를 복원하는 것으로부터 새로운 민중문학의 가능성을 타진한다. 그리고 자매·과부들의 이야기는 추상적 심급에 존재하는 이데올로기보다 훨씬 오래 지속될 것이 분명하다. 언제나 구체적인 삶은 어떠한 이념보다도 오래 지속되는 것이기 때문이다. 그리고 거대 담론에 가리워진 소소한 삶의 결들이야말로 바로 문학의 자리이기 때문이다. 지금 여전히 정지아의 작품이 한국문학의 소중한 자산임은 이 때문이다.

The realities of Korean society continues to be grim, and the role of literature in society remains an important one. However, the efforts to overcome the limitations of past *minjung* literature is found somewhat insufficient. The tendency to consume the legacy of past *minjung* literature as "backstory literature" may lead to the loss of the rich diversity of Korean literature. Jeong Ji-a, on the other hand, begins at the very spot where "The Daughter of the Partisan" began. She finds the future of *minjung* literature at that very place by restoring the narrative of the women who were never given a voice. It is certain that the stories of the widows and sisters will last much longer than the ideologies that exist in abstract court records. The details of life always outlive ideology. And the nooks and crannies of everyday life, overshadowed by the grand narrative, is where literature is located. This is the reason Jeong Ji-a's works are still a valuable asset to Korean literature.

비평의 목소리

Critical Acclaim

생활은 버틴다고 극복되는 것은 아니다. 생활을 통해 다른 것들도 균형 있게 이해할 수 있는 법, 그러나 작가는 이를 그렇게 정리하지 않는다. 남편은 귀가하지 않고 아내는 과거 운동의 동지와 다시 새날을 다짐하고 있다. 말하자면 절대적인 투쟁을 선언하고 있는 셈이며 이는 부부관계에 있어 새로운 모럴의 제시라기보다는 운동에 대한 다짐으로의 비약이다. 말하자면 작은 현실을 쉬운 몸놀림으로 뛰어넘기, 이 점은 정지아의 특징이자 그녀의 힘의 원천이며 작가가 글을 쓰기 시작했던 시기의 분위기를 반영한 것이라고 생각되는 것이다. 바로 혁명적 낙관주의가 그것이다. 서경석

One does not overcome life by sticking it out. One gets a balanced understanding of other aspects of life by examining the everyday. However, Jeong Ji-a does not agree. The husband does not come home, and the wife vows to build a new world with comrades of revolutions past. In other words, this is a declaration of a fundamental fight—a renewed determination for social movement rather than an offering of new morality in marriage. Overcoming a small reality with an easy gesture—this is a Jeong Ji-a characteristic, the source of her power, and a reflection of the times when she began writing. It is a revolutionary optimism. Seo Gyeong-seok

사람들의 시선을 받지 않아도 늘 제자리를 지키며 제
몫의 잎사귀와 열매를 맺는 고욤나무는 힘없고 보잘것
없는 존재들에게도 자기 몫의 생이 있으며 그것 자체만
으로도 찬란하고 아름다울 수 있음을 환기한다. 이렇듯
정지아 소설에 등장하는 인물들은 고욤나무처럼 그 존
재가 미미하지만 오랜 세월을 견디면서 자기 몫의 생을
살아가는 윤리적 감각을 갖춘 인물들이다. 또한 그들은
심해의 물고기가 "납작한 몸과 퇴화된 눈으로 어둠에
잠겨" 있다가 오랜 침잠에서 깨어나 스스로 빛을 발하
듯, 갇힌 일상이나 현재를 억압하는 기억 속을 유영하
다 어느 순간 현실로 솟구치는 인물들이기도 하다.

김양선

야박하고 모진 세상에 빈번히 덜미 잡히며 "비명조차
마음껏 지르지 못"하고 살아온 늙고 상하고 갈 곳 없는
자들의 절규 같은 인생사를 기록하면서도, 정지아는 이
들의 삶을 단지 절망의 서사로 독해하거나 손쉬운 희망
의 서사로 기워내지 않는다. 중얼거림이나 침묵, 때로
는 비명이나 방언으로 된 이들의 말 아닌 말들 속에서
작가는 삶에 대한 그네들의 여전한 열망을 읽어내며,

The date plum, which grows leaves and bears fruit whether anyone cares or not, is a reminder that the plain and downtrodden also have their own lives to live and this fact is in itself brilliant and beautiful. Jeong Ji-a's characters also lead lives as insignificant as those of date plums, but have forged an ethical standard of living that comes from years of hardship. Like fish in the deep ocean floor with its "flat body and obsolete eyes cloaked in darkness" waking up from a long period of obscurity and becoming its own light, they float within the confines of their routines or the memories that oppresses the present and then suddenly make the leap into reality.

Kim Yang-seon

While Jeong Ji-a records the life stories of characters who are old and worn, who lived in a cruel, vicious world that never once granted them room for "a good scream," she does not interpret their stories as a narrative of despair or a convenient message of hope. The writer traces their desires in their mumblings, silences, screams, dialects, and non-verbal expressions, and insists that their slang isn't a monologue but an articulation and entreaty

그들의 언어 아닌 은어들이 독백이 아니라 실은 세상을 향한 말 건넴이며 호소임을 옮겨 쓰고자 한다. 남루한 자들의 열망이란 거창한 사상이 아닌 그저 보잘것없는 '마음'일 것이나, 그 사소하고 하찮은 마음이 되레 사상이 놓치거나 갈라놓은 수다한 마음들을 헤아리고 보듬으며 "기적"을 만들어내기도 하는 것이다.

김경연

aimed at the world. The desires of the weary are nothing grander than a peace of mind, but the focus on feelings assuages the pain overlooked by ideology and creates miracles.

Kim Kyeong-yeon

정지아

정지아는 1965년 전남 구례에서 출생했다. 이후 중앙대학교 문예창작학과에 입학한 후 1990년 빨치산 부모님의 이야기를 소설화한 『빨치산의 딸』을 펴내며 당대 민중문학에 큰 반향을 불러 일으켰다. 그러나 『빨치산의 딸』은 곧 판금 조치를 당하고, 그녀 역시 이후 남한 사회주의노동자동맹(사노맹)의 기관지인 《노동해방문학》 관련 활동으로 수배당한다. 이후 1996년 조선일보 신춘문예에 단편 「고욤나무」가 당선되어 다시 작품 활동을 시작했으며, 2004년에 단편집 『행복』, 2008년에 단편집 『봄빛』을 출간했다. 2006년에 단편 「풍경」으로 제7회 이효석문학상을 수상했으며, 2009년 소설집 『봄빛』으로 제14회 한무숙문학상을 수상했다. 2013년 단편 「숲의 대화」로 제6회 노근리 평화문학상을 수상했다. 현재 중앙대학교 문예창작학과 전공전담교수로 재직 중이다.

Jeong Ji-a

Jeong Ji-a was born in Guryeo, Jeollanam-do in 1965. She wrote *The Daughter of the Partisan* in 1990 when she was a student at the Department of Creative Writing at Chungang University and created a great controversy in the *minjung* literature movement of the time. *The Daughter of the Partisan* was soon banned and she was once a wanted criminal for her participation in the Socialist Laborers' Association magazine, *Labor Liberation Literature*. She resumed her writing career when her short story "Date Plum Tree" won *the Chosun Ilbo* Spring Literary Award in 1996. Short story collections, *Happiness* and *Spring Light* were published in 2004 and 2008 respectively. She won the Yi Hyo-seok Literary Award with her short story, "Scenery" in 2006, and the Han Mu-suk Literary Award with *Spring Light* in 2009. She also received the Nogeun-ri Peace Literary Award with her short story, "Conversations Of A Forest" in 2013. She currently serves as a professor at the Department of Creative Writing at Chungang University.

번역 브랜든 맥케일, 김윤경

Translated by Brendan MacHale and Kim Yoon-kyung

브랜든 맥케일은 1946년 아일랜드에서 출생했고, 1970년 콜롬반 선교사 신부로서 한국에 왔다. 1990년에 영구 귀국했지만, 그 이후로 매년 한국을 방문했다. 1979년에 김동인의 「목숨」을 번역하여 코리아타임즈 문학번역대회에서 장려상을 수상했다. 그 외에 1983년 이범선의 「미친 녀석」과, 2010년 김윤경과 공동 번역한 정지아의 「봄날 오후, 과부 셋」으로 번역상을 수상했다. 그가 번역한 황석영의 「삼포 가는 길」은 1983년 한국 단편소설을 소개한 유네스코 도서에 실린 바 있다.

Brendan MacHale was born in 1946 in Ireland and went to South Korea in 1970 as a Columban missionary priest. He returned home permanently in 1990, though he spends a short time in South Korea every year since. Three short stories appeared in **The Korea Times** literary translation contest: commendation award for Kim Tong-in's "Life" in 1979; overall prize for Lee Pom-son's "The Crazy Fellow" in 1983 and for Jeong Ji-a's "Spring Afternoon, Three Widows" in 2010, a collaborative translation with Kim Yoon-kyung. His translation of Hwang Suk-yong's "The Road to Samp'o" appeared in the UNESCO book of Korean short stories in 1983.

김윤경은 1959년에 서울에서 출생했다. 고려대학교에서 독문학을 전공했으며, 1985년에 석사 학위를 받았다. 결혼 전에 충주대학교에서 강의했으며, 아일랜드로 이민가기 전에 학생들에게 문학과 철학을 가르쳤다.

Born in Seoul, 1959. Studied German Literature at Korea University and got Master degree in Arts in 1985. She worked as a lecturer at Chungju University before marriage, and taught literature and philosophy to young students before her immigration to Ireland.

감수 전승희, 데이비드 윌리엄 홍

Edited by Jeon Seung-hee and David William Hong

전승희는 서울대학교와 하버드대학교에서 영문학과 비교문학으로 박사 학위를 받았으며, 현재 하버드대학교 한국학 연구소의 연구원으로 재직하며 아시아 문예 계간지 《ASIA》 편집위원으로 활동 중이다. 현대 한국문학 및 세계문학을 다룬 논문을 다수 발표했으며, 바흐친의 「장편소설과 민중언어」, 제인 오스틴의 「오만과 편견」 등을 공역했다. 1988년 한국여성연구소의 창립과 《여성과 사회》의 창간에 참여했고, 2002년부터 보스턴 지역 피학대 여성을 위한 단체인 '트랜지션하우스' 운영에 참여해 왔다. 2006년 하버드대학교 한국학 연구소에서 '한국 현대사와 기억'

을 주제로 한 워크숍을 주관했다.

Jeon Seung-hee is a member of the Editorial Board of *ASIA*, and a Fellow at the Korea Institute, Harvard University. She received a Ph.D. in English Literature from Seoul National University and a Ph.D. in Comparative Literature from Harvard University. She has presented and published numerous papers on modern Korean and world literature. She is also a co-translator of Mikhail Bakhtin's *Novel and the People's Culture* and Jane Austen's *Pride and Prejudice*. She is a founding member of the Korean Women's Studies Institute and of the biannual Women's Studies' journal *Women and Society* (1988), and she has been working at 'Transition House,' the first and oldest shelter for battered women in New England. She organized a workshop entitled "The Politics of Memory in Modern Korea" at the Korea Institute, Harvard University, in 2006. She also served as an advising committee member for the Asia-Africa Literature Festival in 2007 and for the POSCO Asian Literature Forum in 2008.

데이비드 윌리엄 홍은 미국 일리노이주 시카고에서 태어났다. 일리노이대학교에서 영문학을, 뉴욕대학교에서 영어교육을 공부했다. 지난 2년간 서울에 거주하면서 처음으로 한국인과 아시아계 미국인 문학에 깊이 몰두할 기회를 가졌다. 현재 뉴욕에서 거주하며 강의와 저술 활동을 한다.

David William Hong was born in 1986 in Chicago, Illinois. He studied English Literature at the University of Illinois and English Education at New York University. For the past two years, he lived in Seoul, South Korea, where he was able to immerse himself in Korean and Asian-American literature for the first time. Currently, he lives in New York City, teaching and writing.

바이링궐 에디션 한국 대표 소설 063
봄날 오후, 과부 셋

2014년 6월 6일 초판 1쇄 인쇄 | 2014년 6월 13일 초판 1쇄 발행

지은이 정지아 | 옮긴이 브랜든 맥케일, 김윤경 | 펴낸이 김재범
감수 전승희, 데이비드 윌리엄 홍 | 기획 정은경, 전성태, 이경재
편집 정수인, 이은혜 | 관리 박신영 | 디자인 이춘희
펴낸곳 (주)아시아 | 출판등록 2006년 1월 27일 제406-2006-000004호
주소 서울특별시 동작구 서달로 161-1(흑석동 100-16)
전화 02.821.5055 | 팩스 02.821.5057 | 홈페이지 www.bookasia.org
ISBN 979-11-5662-018-1 (set) | 979-11-5662-027-3 (04810)
값은 뒤표지에 있습니다.

Bi-lingual Edition Modern Korean Literature 063
Spring Afternoon, Three Widows

Written by Jeong Ji-a | Translated by Brendan MacHale, Kim Yoon-kyung
Published by Asia Publishers | 161-1, Seodal-ro, Dongjak-gu, Seoul, Korea
Homepage Address www.bookasia.org | Tel. (822).821.5055 | Fax. (822).821.5057
First published in Korea by Asia Publishers 2014
ISBN 979-11-5662-018-1 (set) | 979-11-5662-027-3 (04810)

바이링궐 에디션 한국 대표 소설 set 4

디아스포라 Diaspora

가족 Family

유머 Humor